S0-CFM-399

À Élia et Noémie qui ont les plus beaux des sourires !
N. C.

À madame Turpin, ma maîtresse de CP.
H. L. G.

First American Edition 2020
Kane Miller, A Division of EDC Publishing

La Photo de classe des animaux
Published in France in 2019 by L'Élan vert
© 2018 L'Élan vert

All rights reserved. No part of this publication may be reproduced, stored in a retrieval system, or transmitted, in any form or by any means, electronic, mechanical, photocopying, recording or otherwise, without the prior permission of the publisher and copyright owner.

For information contact:
Kane Miller, A Division of EDC Publishing
P.O. Box 470663
Tulsa, OK 74147-0663
www.kanemiller.com
www.edcpub.com
www.usbornebooksandmore.com

Library of Congress Control Number: 2019952229

Manufactured by Regent Publishing Services, Hong Kong
Printed March 2020 in Shenzhen, Guangdong, China

1 2 3 4 5 6 7 8 9 10
ISBN: 978-1-68464-112-3

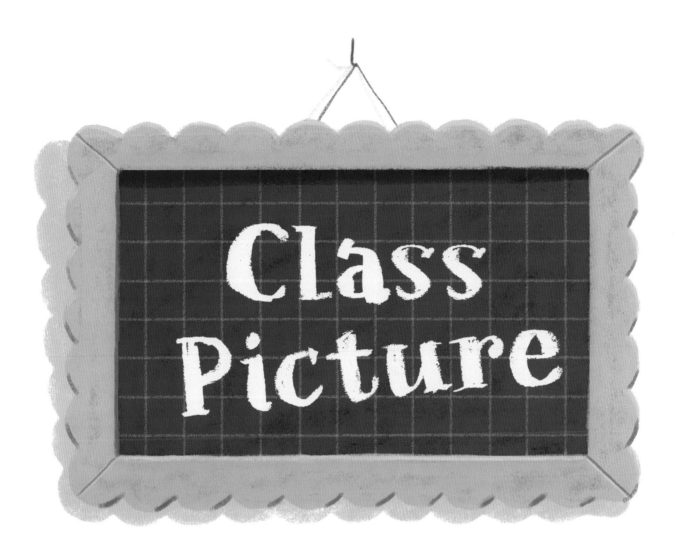

Class Picture

Noé Carlain
Hervé Le Goff

Kane Miller
A DIVISION OF EDC PUBLISHING

The **OSTRICHES** are taking their class picture.

"One, two, three ... everyone, look at the camera!" says the photographer.

The **BEAVERS** are taking their class picture.

"Sit on the bench and ...
Wait, where's the bench?" says the photographer.

The **ELEPHANTS** are taking their class picture.

"Great-grandparents, out of the picture, please,"
says the photographer.

The **HIPPOPOTAMUSES** are taking their class picture.

"Gently, class. Gently ..." says the photographer.

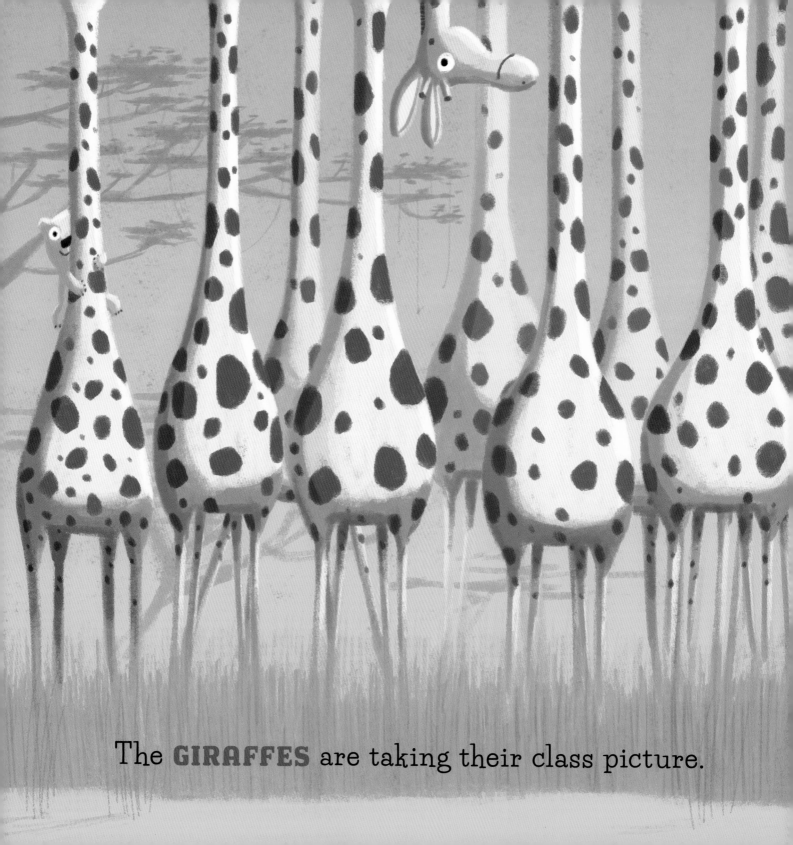

The **GIRAFFES** are taking their class picture.

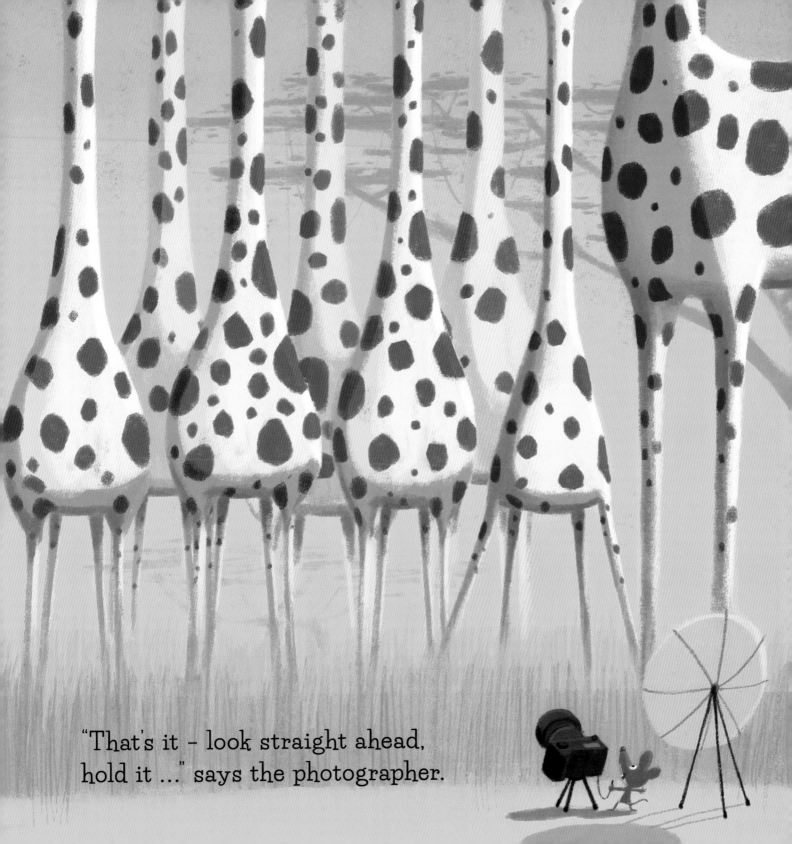

"That's it – look straight ahead,
hold it ..." says the photographer.

The **POLAR BEARS** are taking their class picture.

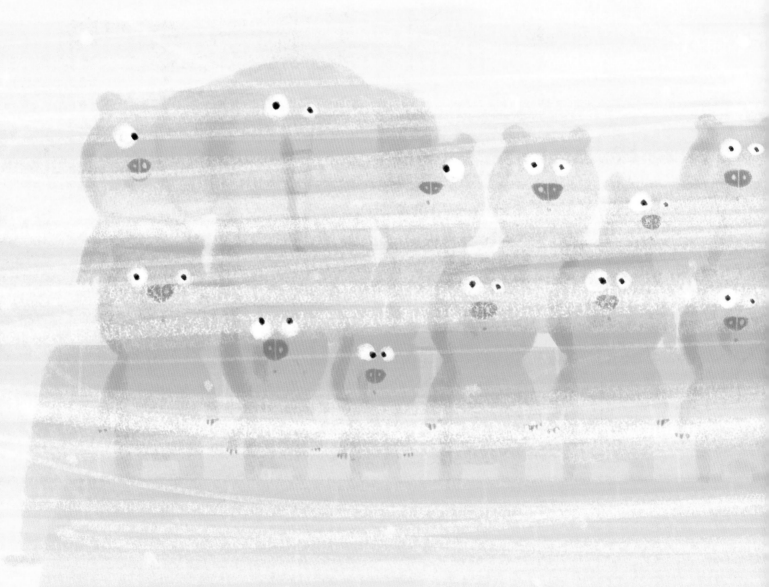

"Is everyone where they're supposed to be?"
says the photographer.

The **RACCOONS** are taking their class picture.

"Is anyone ready?" says the photographer.

The **FOXES** are taking their class picture.

"You can't all be next to your new classmate," says the photographer.

The **SARDINES** are taking their class picture.

"Make room!" says the photographer.

The **SNAKES** are
taking their class picture.

"Will everyone please straighten up,"
says the photographer.

The **MONKEYS** are taking their class picture.

"No more monkeying around!" says the photographer.

"Hooray! Hooray! It's class picture day!"